PLEASE DO NOT
TOUCH THE INDIANS

BY
JOSEPH A. DANDURAND

rENEGADE pLANETS pUBLISHING

Chosen as Small Press Publisher of the Year 2002
by the Wordcraft Circle of Native Writers and Storytellers

Please Do Not Touch The Indians was produced as a Native Voices at the Autry World Premiere March 19-April 4, 2004.

First edition: September 2004
Edited by MariJo Moore and Kathryn Lucci Cooper
Cover art by David P. Bradley, *American Indian Gothic*,
1983, color lithograph on paper
Courtesy Buffalo Bill Historical Center, Cody, Wyoming
Gift of Mrs. D. W. Ethridge
Cover and layout design by Phil Olson

Library of Congress Catalog Card Number: 2004094209
ISBN # 0-9654921-8-4

rENEGADE pLANETS pUBLISHING
PO Box 2493
Candler, NC 28715
Phone: 828-665-7630 * Fax: 828-670-6347
Email renegadepl@aol.com • Website: marijomoore.com

Also by Joseph A. Dandurand

Plays:
Crackers and Soup
No Totem for My Story
Where Two Rivers Meet
Please Do Not Touch the Indians

Poetry:
Upside Down Raven
I Touched the Coyote's Tongue
burning for the dead and scratching for the poor
looking into the eyes of my forgotten dreams
Shake

For my daughters
Danessa Renee Wa yothe and Marlysse Rainyn Dandurand

CHARACTERS

WOODEN INDIAN MAN

WOODEN INDIAN WOMAN

SISTER COYOTE

BROTHER RAVEN

MISTER WOLF

TOURIST

MUSICIAN

SETTING: A PAINTED BACKDROP OF THE HANK WILLIAMS SR'S BAIT AND GIFT SHOP. THERE ARE SOME FALLEN LEAVES ON THE GROUND. CENTRE STAGE THERE IS A WOODEN BENCH AND SITTING ON THE BENCH ARE TWO WOODEN INDIANS. THEIR CLOTHING IS SIMPLE AND NOT QUITE TRADITIONAL BUT MORE OF A HOLLYWOOD TASTE. WOODEN WOMAN IS HOLDING FLOWERS THAT SOMEONE HAS PUT IN HER HAND. WOODEN MAN SITS WITH HIS EYES CLOSED AND AROUND HIS NECK IS A SIGN THAT READS: *PLEASE DO NOT TOUCH THE INDIANS.*

SCENE 1 – DAY

LIGHTS COME UP AS MUSIC BEGINS: HANK WILLIAMS SR'S KALAJAH. MUSIC FADES ON THE LYRICS, "...HAS A HEART OF KNOTTY PINE."

MUSIC ENDS AS A FRENCH TOURIST COMES OUT AND SETS UP A CAMERA AND TRIPOD. FRENCH TOURIST SETS THE TIMER AND SITS BETWEEN THE TWO INDIANS. AS THE TIMER BEEPS, THE WOODEN MAN OPENS HIS EYES, LEANS FORWARD AND STICKS OUT HIS TONGUE. FRENCH TOURIST LOOKS AT WOODEN MAN BUT HE HAS ALREADY RETURNED TO BEING WOODEN. FRENCH TOURIST STANDS, GATHERS THE CAMERA AND TRIPOD, AND EXITS.

SCENE 2 – EVENING

LIGHTS SHIFT TO NIGHT. IN THE DISTANCE WE HEAR SQUEALING TIRES AND SCREAMS FROM TEENAGERS AS THEY CHEER ON THE DRAGGING CARS. WOODEN WOMAN BEGINS TO MOVE AS NOISE FADES. WOODEN WOMAN LOOKS AT FLOWERS IN HER HAND AND SCREAMS AS SHE THROWS THEM TO THE GROUND IN FRONT OF HER.

WOODEN WOMAN
Geez, who put flowers in my hand? Don't they know that's bad luck? Holding flowers is a sign of death. Hey, you listening? Are you awake?

WOODEN MAN DOES NOT MOVE NOR DOES HE SPEAK.

WOODEN WOMAN

You just going to sit there all night and not say a word? Don't you get tired of not moving your mouth? Geez, I'd go crazy not being able to talk. You better move your mouth or else you'll never be able to talk. That's what happen to old Charlie Ketchup. He never spoke to a soul for the last twenty years of his life. When the doctor went to see him on his death bed, Charlie couldn't even tell him where it hurt. I bet he's talking up a storm in the spirit world. Old Charlie Ketchup. I knew his wife, she was crazier than he was. Betty Ketchup. A big woman, she must of weighed about three hundred pounds. No wonder Charlie never spoke, she'd come screaming out of the house after him if he ever spoke a word against her. Never seen a woman move so fast, never seen a man move faster.

WOODEN MAN SCRATCHES HIS NOSE.

WOODEN WOMAN

Betty Ketchup sure was a big woman, but she would never hurt anyone. I remember going to her house to borrow some wood one day and she was running around trying to catch every fly that came into her dirty house. I'd say, "What'cha doing with them flies, Betty Ketchup?" And she'd turn and look at me with that little mouth of hers trying so hard to suck in enough air to breath, and she'd say, "I'm catchin' em' for my supper." And she'd laugh so hard, I was always afraid she'd swallow more than she caught.

WOODEN MAN SCRATCHES HIS LEFT KNEE.

WOODEN WOMAN

She never did eat any of them. She was really catching them because she could never kill a fly. She'd spend the whole day catching them and storing them in an old jar that she kept on the kitchen sink right next to her set of teeth. I followed her one day, you know to see where she went with them flies. She must've had a hundred in that jar that day. She waddled her way to the cow field and here she came across the biggest cow patty that she could find. It was real fresh, the steam still rising. Betty Ketchup opened up her jar of flies and let them fly right on to the patty. A hundred flies with a new home. Those flies never came back to Betty Ketchup's house. They stayed on that cow patty for the rest of their lives. Betty Ketchup saved millions of lives in the ten years that I knew her. Never a dead fly in her dirty kitchen. A place to live was all they wanted. She was a big woman and her heart was just as big.

LIGHTS FADE AS A COYOTE BARKS.

SCENE 3 – NIGHT

MORE LEAVES FALL TO THE GROUND. WOODEN MAN SNAPS AWAKE AND REALIZES HE HAS A CHEAP VINYL HEADRESS ON HIS HEAD. HE TAKES IT OFF AND LOOKS DOWN AT THE SIGN AROUND HIS NECK: *PLEASE DO NOT TOUCH THE INDIANS.* **HE STARES AT WOODEN WOMAN AS HE TAKES OFF THE SIGN AND PUTS IT UNDER THE BENCH.**

WOODEN MAN

Are you awake? I had a vision: I was on the river, my boat was filled with fish, I had started home when a coyote began to follow me from the shore, he was smilin' at me, you know, with them yellow eyes, he's smilin' with his crooked teeth. He took his time, stopping every so often to rest his ragged paws, he knew my boat couldn't get very far with all that fish. My boat was pushing slowly up to our home, the coyote watched from the shore and then the raven came and joined the coyote, they both watched from the shore: the raven with his red eyes and his torn feathers, the coyote lights a cigarette and blows the smoke towards me and my boat. The raven smiles as coyote offers him a drag. They both sit there on a log and they laugh at me. The fish begin to dance, they want to go back to the river, they do not want to be eaten by the coyote nor do they want to be picked at by the raven. The fish begin to sing to me, they tell me to throw them back: "Please throw us back, we will come back next year." Over and over they sing this to me. The raven and the coyote are laughing at me as they begin to share their bottle. And then I begin to throw the fish back to the river, the fish throw kisses to me as they swim back to their homes, they promise to name their children after me, they turn and disappear. The raven and the coyote stand there on shore, their mouths open with confusion. They try and catch up to me but my boat is empty and goes like the wind. I hear them howlin' and cawing at me as I disappear around the mountain... I don't think they will name their children after me I thought to myself and then I woke up. Hey, are you awake? Did you like the flowers?

SCENE 4A -DAY

AN ENGLISH TOURIST ENTERS AND SETS UP A CAMERA. HE SETS
THE TIMER AND SITS BETWEEN THE WOODEN INDIANS. AS THE
TIMER BEEPS, THE WOODEN MAN AND WOODEN WOMAN
REACH BEHIND THE TOURIST WITH "RABBIT EAR" GESTURES.
BOTH INDIANS SNAP BACK TO BEING WOODEN AS ENGLISH
TOURIST LOOKS AT THEM AS IF THEY DID TRULY MOVE. HE
SHAKES HIS HEAD, GOES TO GATHER HIS CAMERA AND EXITS.

IN THE LIGHT SHIFT, WE HEAR A COYOTE BARK FOLLOWED BY
A VOICE YELLING: "GET OUT OF HERE, YOU STINKING
COYOTE!" A SPOT COMES UP DOWNSTAGE CENTRE. SISTER
COYOTE ENTERS CRYING. SHE IS BEAUTIFUL BUT HER MAKE-
UP HAS RUN DOWN HER FACE SO NOW SHE LOOKS SOMEWHAT
CLOWNISH AND SAD. SISTER COYOTE REACHES INTO HER
PURSE AND PULLS OUT A CIGARETTE, LIGHTS IT, TAKES A HUGE
DRAG AND EXHALES IT INTO THE AIR. SHE DOES THIS AGAIN
AND TRIES TO ACT COOL AND SPECIAL BUT INHALES DOWN
THE WRONG PIPE AND BEGINS TO CHOKE AND HER EYES BUG
OUT AND SHE APPEARS EVEN MORE CLOWNISH THAN BEFORE.

SISTER COYOTE
Nothing like a good smoke. You know I first started smoking when me
and my sister went to the carnival that would come to our reserve every
summer. We really went with our parents but as soon as we got there we
would run away and disappear into the crowd and our parents were going
to the beer-tent anyways so they didn't miss us much. We would run straight
for the far end of the carnival grounds. You see this is where the freaks and
the scary rides were all kept.

SHE PUTS THE CIGARETTE OUT AND PUTS IT BACK INTO THE
PACK IN HER PURSE AND SMILES. SHE DIGS INTO HER PURSE
FOR A COMPACT AND BEGINS TO FIX HER MAKE-UP.

SISTER COYOTE
My sister and I had both started to wear make-up, not very well I may add, not
like I wear mine now. We didn't know a thing back then but we didn't care
because we were thirteen and we were away from the reserve for a day and we
had a pack of Marlboros that we had stolen from dad and we were looking to
smoke and act cool and we were looking to see if there were any cute guys that
had come with the carnival. We didn't see any, they were all fat ugly guys with
a lot of tattoos and they smelled like horses. We walked around and smoked

and we ate junk food and sipped cokes and we walked like we owned this land, well we did, well our people did, but we walked like we owned it and we let people know that we were smoking and we were cool.

SISTER COYOTE
As the day wore on and the sun got hot and we became kind of sick from all the food and the pop and the Marlboros, my sister said she was going to find mom and dad and I went to check out more of the freak shows and maybe see if there were any cute guys hiding in the Haunted House. I was making my way towards the Haunted House when I saw IT.

WOODEN MAN REACTS TO THE STORY.

SISTER COYOTE
There it was in big red letters on a black sign: SEE THE TWO-HEADED BABY. I freaked out. I reached into my pocket and dug for the quarter that I knew was there and then I ran up the stairs that led to the TWO-HEADED BABY. When I got to the top of the stairs a man who smelled like horses took my quarter and told me to go on in and to leave out the other side when I had had enough. I went in and it was dark and smelled like horses and over in the corner there was a table and on the table there was a jar and in the jar was the TWO-HEADED BABY. And I walked up to it and I looked at it and it turned and it looked at me. I screamed but no one could hear me over all the noise on the rides outside. I wanted to run but I couldn't look away so I stood there and it stared back at me and I stared back at it. I moved closer to see if it was really alive but how could it be alive, right? I mean it was floating in some sort of liquid in a jar and it was a two-headed baby, so how could it have lived in the first place, right? But when I went up to it, it moved again but not real movement more like floating movement like it was in space or something and it just spun around and around inside that jar and I just stared at it and stared at it and as its heads would spin around, the eyes would stare at me and they were looking at me like they wanted to come out of that jar and play.

WOODEN MAN REACHES UNDERNEATH THE BENCH AND TAKES OUT AN OLD BASEBALL GLOVE AND BALL.

SISTER COYOTE
I wanted to run and I wanted to scream but I just stood there and stared and then someone else came in and they wanted to stare at the two-headed baby and I let them and I went outside and I never went back and as I went down the stairs I threw up all over some cute guy who was combing the BEARDED LADY'S beard.

WOODEN MAN DROPS THE BALL AND IT ROLLS OVER BESIDE SISTER COYOTE. LIGHTS BRIGHTEN AS SHE PICKS UP THE BALL AND WALKS TOWARDS THE WOODEN MAN.

SISTER COYOTE
You dropped your ball.

WOODEN MAN STARES AT HER AND HOLDS UP HIS GLOVE FOR HER TO THROW HIM THE BALL.

WOODEN MAN
I could never throw a curve ball. All my life I couldn't throw a curve to save it.

SISTER COYOTE
I could show you mine. I was pitcher for the REDHAWKS. We were the meanest team you ever set eyes on.

WOODEN MAN STANDS AND TOSSES HER THE BALL.

WOODEN MAN
My dad tried to show me how to throw a curve but the ball just wouldn't curve for me. He'd get so mad, his face would get all white and he would spit a little out of the corner of his mouth and he would swear and go in the house and turn the TV on and he would mumble: "Kid's arm is useless."

SISTER COYOTE WALKS OVER TO THE OPPOSITE SIDE OF THE STAGE AND FACES HIM AS SHE TOSSES THE BALL UP INTO THE AIR AND FEELS IT IN THE PALM OF HER HAND. SHE SCRATCHES OUT HER MOUND WITH HER FOOT AND SHE READIES HERSELF TO THROW A PITCH.

SISTER COYOTE
Our coach was the chief and he made the rules because he bought all the uniforms and he supplied the equipment. He pretended like he was BIG LEAGUE but he didn't know a thing about baseball and the only thing BIG about him was his belly and his big belly stuck out of his shirt and he would just sit in the dugout and pretend like he was giving us secret signals. We all would look at him and pretend that he was running the show but really it was Lucy the third baseman who was making the calls and she called for a fastball and I would wind up and give her my best fastball.

SHE THROWS HIM A FASTBALL WITH SOME SMOKE BEHIND IT AND IT MAKES A HARD SNAPPING SOUND AS IT HITS THE GLOVE.

WOODEN MAN
Strike One!

WOODEN MAN TOSSES IT BACK AT HER AND RESUMES HIS CATCHER POSITION. SHE DOES HER RITUAL AND PREPARES HERSELF FOR ANOTHER PITCH. WOODEN MAN READIES HIMSELF AGAIN FOR THE NEXT PITCH. SHE THROWS IT AND IT HITS THE GLOVE JUST LIKE THE FIRST ONE.

WOODEN MAN
Strike Two!

HE STANDS UP AND WALKS TOWARDS HER AS IF HE IS THE CATCHER WALKING TOWARDS THE MOUND IN AN IMPORTANT GAME. HE GIVES HER THE BALL AND KICKS AT THE DIRT.

SISTER COYOTE
Ok, I've given two of my best pitches and all I have left is my curve and I've been working hard on it all week but it just sort of hangs there and doesn't curve that much and the chief is getting all mad and he's threatening to pull me out of the game and all my friends are there and that cute guy in grade twelve is there with all his friends and he's come to see my great curve ball and this is the time for it, right?

WOODEN MAN
The CURVE.

HE WALKS SLOWLY BACK TO HOME PLATE AS SHE CONTINUES TO TALK TO HERSELF.

SISTER COYOTE
Was there any other choice? You had thrown the fastball on the first pitch and that batter just sat there and she knew yes she knew that the curve was coming up, everyone knew that the curve was going to be the last pitch, so she just sat there and she chewed her big wad of gum and she just waited for the third pitch because she knew it was going to be my weakest pitch.

WOODEN MAN CROUCHES IN HIS CATCHER POSITION AND HE SMACKS THE DUST OUT OF HIS GLOVE AND READIES HIMSELF FOR THE NEXT PITCH. SISTER COYOTE WINDS UP, CHECKS THE BASES, LOOKS BACK AT THE CATCHER AND SHE THROWS THE MOST PERFECT CURVE BALL THAT SHE COULD EVER THROW AND IT HITS THE GLOVE WITH A RESOUNDING SMACK.

WOODEN MAN
Strike three, you're out!

SISTER COYOTE
It was the most beautiful pitch that I have ever thrown in my life, even now I could never have thrown a better pitch and everyone was screaming and yelling at me like I was some sort of hero and the girls on my team all ran up to me and they put me on their shoulders and paraded me up and down the third base line and all the people in the stands cheered and called out my name and the cute guy in grade twelve smiled to me and gave me the thumbs up sign and the chief was trying to get at me and hug me but he tripped and ripped the seat of his uniform pants and everyone saw his bum and everyone started to laugh at him and he began to laugh and everyone was laughing, even the other team who had traveled all this way to try and beat us but we had beaten them, yes, we had beaten them with the best curve ball anyone could've thrown on that day.

WOODEN MAN
Nice pitch, kid.

HE WALKS OVER AND SITS DOWN IN HIS SPOT AND PUTS THE GLOVE AND BALL BACK UNDERNEATH THE BENCH AND STARTS TO BECOME WOODEN. SISTER COYOTE CROSSES TO HIM AND HANDS HIM BACK THE BASEBALL GLOVE.

SISTER COYOTE
Arm's a little tired. Not used to the distance, I guess.

SHE SITS DOWN AT THE FEET OF THE WOODEN MAN AND LEANS AGAINST HIS LEGS AS SHE GOES TO SLEEP.

WOODEN MAN
Nice pitch, kid.

AS STAGE LIGHTS BEGIN TO FADE TO NIGHT, WE HEAR A RAVEN CAWING FOLLOWED BY A VOICE YELLING: "GET OUT OF HERE, YOU STINKING RAVEN!" BROTHER RAVEN STUMBLES IN, SETTLES HIMSELF AND LIGHTS A CIGARETTE. HE THEN TAKES A DRAG.

BROTHER RAVEN
I was picking at the apples in the garbage. Just picking at the apples. Where is the wrong in that?

TAKES ANOTHER LONG DRAG AND IT GOES DOWN THE WRONG PIPE AND HE BEGINS TO COUGH. HE CAREFULLY PUTS THE CIGARETTE OUT AND SAVES IT FOR LATER.

BROTHER RAVEN
Never was much of a smoker.

BROTHER RAVEN TAKES A BOTTLE OUT OF HIS JACKET AND TAKES A GOOD SIZE SWIG.

BROTHER RAVEN
Now drinking is more of my style. Nothing like a good shot to get the earth moving. Nothing like a good shot.

MORE LEAVES FALL TO THE GROUND. BROTHER RAVEN SITS DOWN AND TAKES A PIECE OF PAPER AND A PIECE OF CANDY FROM A FLAT POUCH IN HIS POCKET. HE UNWRAPS THE CANDY, ADMIRES IT, THEN PUTS IT INTO HIS MOUTH AND SAVOURS THE SWEET TASTE AS HE UNCRUMPLES THE PIECE OF PAPER AND BEGINS TO READ IT.

BROTHER RAVEN
"In the morning as mother walked to the river and all the children slept so peaceful on the floor with their little feet sticking out of the warm blankets, there would be a calm quietness that came over the land and all you could hear was the river as it moved gently to the ocean and mother would walk down to the river and she would take off her dress and she would slip into the water and bathe herself and ready herself for the long day ahead."

HE TAKES THE CANDY OUT OF HIS MOUTH AND GENTLY PUTS IT BACK IN THE WRAPPER AND CONTINUES TO READ FROM THE PIECE OF PAPER.

BROTHER RAVEN

"Mother would start the fire and me and my brothers and sisters would rise up off the floor and stare at her in wonderment and she would ask us if we had had any visions in our sleep and I would always answer yes and proceed to tell her what I had seen: I had seen a young salmon come to the shore from the river and it whispered to me that I should join her in the water and I asked her why and she giggled and said it was nice and warm, so I went in and the salmon swam right beside me and she would whisper to me that I was cute and that I had skinny legs and I would laugh and try and catch her but she was a salmon and she could swim somewhat better than I could and she would always get away before I could touch her. Mother would always laugh at my visions and my brothers and sisters would always laugh and tease me and they would always show me the salmon they had caught and say to me: "Is this her, is this her!" And I would cry because what if it was her and they had cut her open and they had put her on the fire and I had eaten her. Mother would try and explain to them what my visions meant but they were too eager to run out and play in the forest and I would just sit there and mother would tell me her visions and I would eat tuna sandwiches because I felt too bad about eating salmon and mother would join me on the floor and hold me tight and she would laugh as she told her visions and I would laugh too because she was so funny and kind, so funny and kind."

HE FOLDS UP PIECE OF PAPER AND PUTS IT BACK INTO HIS POCKET AS STAGE LIGHTS COME UP AND WOODEN WOMAN BEGINS TO MOVE. SHE REACHES BENEATH THE BENCH AND PULLS OUT A HORSE TOY AND BEGINS TO PLAY WITH IT, TRYING TO GET BROTHER RAVEN'S ATTENTION.

BROTHER RAVEN

Always had the ability to have visions. Never know quite what they mean but they mean something and I have them every night.

BROTHER RAVEN BEGINS TO GATHER HIS THINGS. WOODEN WOMAN STOPS PLAYING WITH THE TOY AND REACHES UNDERNEATH THE BENCH AGAIN AND THIS TIME SHE COMES OUT WITH A BAG OF MARBLES.

BROTHER RAVEN

Just picking at the apples. Never meant any harm to no one but they think you're stealing from them even if the apples are rotten. Even if the apples are rotten...

WOODEN WOMAN CROSSES TOWARD BROTHER RAVEN, SHAKING THE BAG OF MARBLES TO GET HIS ATTENTION. BROTHER RAVEN STANDS AND NOTICES HER.

WOODEN WOMAN
Play for funsies or keepsies?

BROTHER RAVEN
Keepsies.

WOODEN WOMAN
Ok, ok, but I get to shoot first and you can't say funsies if I start to win, all right?

BROTHER RAVEN
All right, but I only have one marble and if I lose it I can't play anymore.

WOODEN WOMAN
Ok, you better shoot first. Where's your marble?

HE REACHES INTO HIS POCKET AND PULLS OUT A RED MARBLE. HE HOLDS IT UP TO THE LIGHT AND STARES THROUGH IT. WOODEN WOMAN COMES UP BESIDE HIM AND SHE STARES THROUGH IT TOO.

WOODEN WOMAN
It's lovely.

BROTHER RAVEN
It's the prettiest marble I've ever owned. All my life I've been playing marbles and this is the prettiest one I've ever come across.

WOODEN WOMAN
All red and you can see right through it.

HE BRINGS IT DOWN FROM THE LIGHT AND STEPS BACK AWAY FROM HER AND KNEELS DOWN AND READIES HIMSELF TO PLAY MARBLES. WOODEN WOMAN KNEELS DOWN BESIDE HIM AND LOOKS HIM RIGHT IN THE EYES.

WOODEN WOMAN
Where did you get that marble?

BROTHER RAVEN
I'm not supposed to say.

WOODEN WOMAN
Why not? Is it a magic marble? Because if it is then I don't want to play for keepsies.

BROTHER RAVEN
Too late.

HE BEGINS TO WIN ALL HER MARBLES. SHE KNEELS THERE BESIDE HIM AND WATCHES AS HE MAKES THE MOST AMAZING SHOTS SHE HAS EVER SEEN. THE RED MARBLE BANKS AND KICKS OUT ALL HER MARBLES, AND SHE SITS THERE IN WONDERMENT. HE COLLECTS ALL HER MARBLES AND BEGINS TO PUT THEM IN HIS POUCH.

WOODEN WOMAN
No fair. Winning with a magic marble just isn't fair.

BROTHER RAVEN
Here, have an apple.

HE REACHES INTO HIS POCKET AND OFFERS HER ONE OF HIS ROTTEN APPLES, AND SHE TAKES IT AND BITES INTO IT WITHOUT LOOKING AT IT.

WOODEN WOMAN
Good apple.

BROTHER RAVEN
I picked it myself.

WOODEN WOMAN
I was good at picking cherries.

BROTHER RAVEN
Not me. I couldn't climb the trees and I was always falling out of them and landing on my head. I just ate the ones that fell to the ground.

WOODEN WOMAN CROSSES TO BROTHER RAVEN AND LIFTS HER DRESS UP TO THE KNEE. BROTHER RAVEN KNEELS AT HER FEET.

WOODEN WOMAN
See this scar right here on my calf. A spirit gave me that scar. You see, I got that one from falling down a cherry tree when I was just a little girl. The tree was on Old Irving's land. No one ever went on to his land because everyone thought his land was full of bad spirits. They used to say the spirits were bad because they had all died on the same day and they had all died on the same hour and they had all died the same way and they had all been buried together on Irving's land. No one ever went on his land. No one ever dared.

BROTHER RAVEN GETS COMFORTABLE TO HEAR HER STORY.

WOODEN WOMAN
Nothing on his land but rocks and weeds anyways so we pretty much stayed away from him and his land of bad spirits. But there was that cherry tree that everyone knew and talked about. They said that the cherries were so big and juicy that you could eat one and be full for a week. They said this tree never went a day without a new cherry growing and becoming big and juicy. As you can tell by this scar I went on that land and I went past those bad spirits and I went up that cherry tree and I picked me the biggest and the juiciest of all the cherries on the earth. I ate maybe four or five and stuck the rest of them cherries into my pockets and I was making my way down the tree when I saw her.

BROTHER RAVEN MOVES TO GET MORE COMFORTABLE AS HE IS LULLED INTO SLEEP.

WOODEN WOMAN
I've never seen such a sight in all my life. It was a young girl. She looked to be maybe ten or eleven. She stood there at the bottom of the tree and she looked up at me. I spoke to her and I said: "Hey, would you like some cherries?" The little girl stared at me and then she touched the tree and the whole tree shook, no, the whole world felt like it was shaking and I tried to hold on but I couldn't because my hands were slippery from the juiciest cherries in the whole wide world and I fell, no, I slid all the way down that tree and fell right at her feet. That girl just stared at me as I ran, no, I limped all the way off of Irving's land and I never looked back. So you see, a spirit gave me this scar.

BROTHER RAVEN FALLS COMPLETELY ASLEEP AND AS HE DOES THIS HIS MAGIC RED MARBLE FALLS OUT OF HIS HAND AND WOODEN WOMAN REACHES DOWN AND PICKS IT UP AND SHE STARES AT IT IN THE LIGHT AS STAGE LIGHTS BEGIN TO FADE.

WOODEN WOMAN
Finders keepers.

LIGHTS SHIFT AS A WOLF HOWLS. WOODEN WOMAN GATHERS BROTHER RAVEN TO SLEEP AT HER FEET JUST LIKE SISTER COYOTE IS SITTING WITH THE WOODEN MAN, THEN SHE BECOMES WOODEN AGAIN.

SCENE 5

A GERMAN TOURIST ENTERS AND SETS UP A CAMERA ON A TRIPOD. SISTER COYOTE IS ASLEEP ON ONE SIDE OF THE BENCH AND BROTHER RAVEN IS ASLEEP ON THE OTHER SIDE. WOODEN MAN AND WOODEN WOMAN ARE IN THEIR USUAL SPOTS ON THE BENCH. THE GERMAN TOURIST SETS THE TIMER AND CROSSES TO STAND BEHIND THE TWO WOODEN INDIANS ON THE BENCH. WHEN THE TIMER BEEPS THE GERMAN TOURIST SMILES AND THE WOODEN MAN AND WOMAN STICK OUT THEIR TONGUES BEFORE QUICKLY GOING WOODEN AGAIN. THE GERMAN TOURIST LOOKS AT THE WOODEN MAN AND WOODEN WOMAN. HE SHAKES HIS HEAD AND THEN CROSSES TO GATHER HIS CAMERA AND TRIPOD AND EXITS.

SISTER COYOTE MOVES AND TALKS IN HER SLEEP.

SISTER COYOTE
Tell me a story, Poppa. Tell me a story, Poppa.

WOODEN MAN LOOKS DOWN AT HER.

WOODEN MAN
Are you talking to me? Cause if you are then you should look me in the eyes, not polite to ask someone for something and not look them in the eyes.

SISTER COYOTE CHILDISHLY COVERS HER EYES. WOODEN MAN STANDS AS HE CONTINUES TO SPEAK TO HER.

WOODEN MAN

I met a man once who wouldn't look me in the eyes. He'd always be wanting something from me and he would come right up to my door and he'd ask for it without ever looking me in the eyes and I'd tell him "No" every time and he'd walk away all mad but he would come back and he would ask me for something else and I would look him right in the eyes and I knew that I would give him whatever it was he was asking for if he would just have the respect to look me in the eyes when he asked for it, but he never did and I'd tell him "No" and he hated me. That man hated me because I asked for respect.

SISTER COYOTE MOVES AGAIN AND MUMBLES SLEEPILY.

WOODEN MAN

So I'm talking to you because there's no one else to talk to right now and I have to tell you about this vision I just had and if I don't tell anyone then I think I may have to scream and if you've ever heard me scream then you know what a loud scream that I have. So here is my vision. I was on...

SISTER COYOTE

Poppa? You there, Poppa? The house is so cold and all the wood is still wet and my blanket's too small cause I'm getting taller. Can you see that I'm getting taller, Poppa?

WOODEN MAN

Listen, if we're going to have a conversation then you'll have to respect that I was talking and it was my turn to tell you about my vision, so you just sit there and not say a word, all right? All right. Anything more to say before I carry on with my vision? No?

SHE SHAKES HER HEAD.

WOODEN MAN

I was on the river. I know, I know, I am always on the river but this time I was really on the river. I was born on the river, I bet you didn't know that. I was born and raised on that river.

SISTER COYOTE

Poppa, can I have another piece of bread? My belly isn't quite full yet.

HE TURNS AND STARES AT HER UNTIL SHE SETTLES IN TO LISTEN TO HIM.

WOODEN MAN

I was on the river and I was on my old boat. That old boat sure could move when it wanted to. It could cut through the water and nothing, no storm, no wind, could stop her from getting me home.

SISTER COYOTE MOVES TO GET MORE COMFORTABLE.

WOODEN MAN

I was on the river and I was on my old boat and we were heading home from a long day of fishing. I didn't pull in too much on that day but I had enough for supper. The water was calm and there was no wind on that day and you could just make out the blue of the sky and you could just catch a glimpse of the mountains. We were making real good time when all of a sudden the engine went dead. I tried to start it up again but she just wouldn't turn.

WE HEAR RAIN AND WIND AS HE CONTINUES.

WOODEN MAN

Then the wind came out of nowhere and the rain started to fall hard and the blue of the sky was gone and it was dark and you could no longer see the mountains and the boat turned and started to head down river as the river's current became strong and angry. I had no idea where I was anymore. The boat seemed to have a life of its own and it took me where it wanted to go and I had to go because there was no choice and the boat landed itself on shore and then the wind stopped and the rain stopped and the sky cleared and there was the blue and there was the mountains and I still had no idea where I was.

WIND AND RAIN SOUNDS STOP. OFFSTAGE WE HEAR A WOLF HOWLING FOLLOWED BY A VOICE SAYING: "GET OUT OF HERE, YOU STINKING WOLF!" MISTER WOLF WALKS IN, HE IS DRESSED IN A THREE-PIECE SUIT AND HE IS WEARING SUNGLASSES.

WOODEN MAN

I got off the boat and went down the shoreline trying to figure out where I was but nothing was familiar to me and it felt like I was in a different world and then I saw him. He was sitting on a log and he had a cigarette and smiled right at me.

WOODEN MAN LOOKS AT MISTER WOLF AS HE LIGHTS A CIGARETTE AND BLOWS THE SMOKE INTO THE AIR AS HE SMILES.

MISTER WOLF
That your boat?

WOODEN MAN
Yes it is. It's a good...

MISTER WOLF
I need a boat.

WOODEN MAN
She's not for sale.

MISTER WOLF
Did I say I wanted to buy a boat?

WOODEN MAN
No.

MISTER WOLF
No, I did not. I said I needed a boat. Is this one available?

WOODEN MAN
I was going home and the wind brought me here. I have to get home and cook the fish before they go bad. If you like I could take you up river a ways.

MISTER WOLF
That would be fine.

WOODEN MAN MOVES AS IF TO GET IN A BOAT. MISTER WOLF PUTS HIS CIGARETTE OUT AND TAKES OFF HIS SUNGLASSES AND PUTS THEM INTO HIS POCKET THEN CROSSES TO WOODEN MAN.

WOODEN MAN
This vision feels so real.

MISTER WOLF
What? What did you say?

LIGHTNING STRIKES - A STORM ENSUES

WOODEN MAN
Nothing. You must've heard that thunder. It's been real crazy today.

MISTER WOLF
Can't this heap go any faster?

WOODEN MAN
She usually goes faster but her belly is full of fish that I caught today. See.

MISTER WOLF LOOKS BESIDE HIM AND PRETENDS TO PICK UP FISH AND EAT THEM WHOLE UNTIL THEY ARE ALL GONE. WOODEN MAN WHISPERS TO SISTER COYOTE, WOODEN WOMAN AND BROTHER RAVEN.

WOODEN MAN
He is eating all my fish. There must've been thirty fish in her belly and he is eating them all. He is eating them whole.

MISTER WOLF STANDS, FEELS HIS FULL BELLY AND LETS OUT A LONG BURP.

MISTER WOLF
Now you can go faster.

WOODEN MAN IS ANGRY BECAUSE MISTER WOLF HAS EATEN ALL HIS FISH.

WOODEN MAN
You want to go fast, well here we go!

WOODEN MAN GRABS MISTER WOLF BY THE HAND AND DRAGS HIM AROUND THE STAGE AS IF GOING FAST ON A BOAT. THEY BUILD AND BUILD THEIR ACTIONS UNTIL THEY CRASH INTO ONE ANOTHER CENTER STAGE, CAUSING WOODEN MAN TO FALL

MISTER WOLF
Where am I?

WOODEN MAN
I've got to stop having them visions. They're really getting kind of weird.

MISTER WOLF
Where am I?

WOODEN MAN STANDS AND LIMPS BACK TO SIT DOWN IN USUAL SPOT.

WOODEN MAN
You're right here. Where else would you be?

MISTER WOLF STARES AT HIM.

MISTER WOLF
Do I know you?

WOODEN MAN WHISPERS TO SISTER COYOTE WHO IS STILL ON THE GROUND BESIDE THE BENCH.

WOODEN MAN
Watch this one, he's very tricky.

THE GROUP BECOMES WOODEN AS MISTER WOLF CROSSES TO THE BENCH.

MISTER WOLF
What? I didn't hear what you said. You're going to have to speak up because I seem to have lost some of my hearing.

MISTER WOLF GOES UP TO WOODEN MAN AND TAPS HIM BUT WOODEN MAN DOES NOT MOVE. HE SNIFFS SISTER COYOTE THEN SNIFFS WOODEN MAN AND SNEEZES. NEXT HE SNIFFS WOODEN WOMAN AND SMILES. HE CANNOT GET THEM TO RESPOND. HE GIVES UP AND CROSSES TO THE PLATFORM AS LIGHTS SHIFT.

MISTER WOLF
Right back to where I began. No one to talk to. No one to laugh and play tricks on. Just me and the earth.

REACHES INTO HIS POCKET AND PULLS OUT AN OLD POCKET WATCH AND CHAIN. HE STARES AT IT AND HE LISTENS TO SEE IF IT STILL TICKS.

MISTER WOLF
Never know if it's the right time or not. Can't tell by this old timepiece. It's only good to stare at when the sun is out. See how it glows in the light.

HE HOLDS IT UP TO THE LIGHT AND WATCHES IT AS IT SPINS AND GLEAMS IN THE LIGHT.

MISTER WOLF
Never was good for telling the right time.

HE PUTS THE WATCH BACK INTO HIS POCKET.

MISTER WOLF
Always had clocks and timepieces for the time at any time in my life. When I was a kid we had two clocks, one in the kitchen on top of the stove and one in Grandma's room right next to her bed. You could hear that old clock ticking just as loud as Grandma's snoring. We used to sneak in there at night and set the alarm to ring at exactly midnight and wait for it to ring and for Grandma to wake up and scream at us kids to stop fooling around but we would be laughing so hard and she would start giggling too and swear up and down that all us kids were crazy and that we should be locked up somewhere. We would get Grandma a tea and let her get back to sleep and we would go on to our rooms which were on the other side of the kitchen and we would pass the other clock that was on the stove and it would tell us that it was bedtime and we would all go to sleep and we would all hear the ticking of them two clocks because one was faster than the other: tick tick tock tock tick tick tock tock...

HE CURLS UP AND GOES TO SLEEP AS LIGHTS BEGIN TO FADE.

SCENE 6

IN THE NIGHT WE HEAR HORSES AND MEN SCREAMING: CHARGE! LIGHTS SHIFT TO DAY. WOODEN MAN AND WOODEN WOMAN ARE SITTING IN THEIR PLACE ON THE BENCH, SISTER COYOTE SITS TO THE RIGHT OF WOODEN MAN, BROTHER RAVEN IS STANDING TO THE LEFT OF WOODEN WOMAN, MISTER WOLF IS STANDING BEHIND. THEY HOLD THEIR POSE AS THE TOURIST, NOW DRESSED AS A MOUNTIE, ENTERS AND SETS UP HIS CAMERA AND TRIPOD. HE SETS THE TIMER AND GOES BEHIND THE BENCH AND PUTS HIS HAT ON MISTER WOLF'S HEAD. AS THE TIMER BEEPS THE TOURIST RAISES HIS HAND AND MAKES THE PEACE SYMBOL. ALL THE OTHER CHARACTERS EACH RAISE ONE OF THEIR MIDDLE FINGERS THEN QUICKLY BECOME WOODEN AGAIN. TOURIST LOOKS AT EACH OF THEM AS IF THEY DID MOVE, SHAKES HIS HEAD AND GATHERS HIS CAMERA AND EXITS.

WOODEN MAN
He smelled like horseshit!

SISTER COYOTE
He must've stepped in it when he got off his horse.

MISTER WOLF
Smells more like he was rolling around in it, you know they do that.

BROTHER RAVEN
Do they really?

MISTER WOLF
Sure they do. Some sort of ritual. Some sort of ceremony to make them stronger when they go into battle.

WOODEN MAN
He's going to scare the other side away smelling like that. They won't be able to see him coming because he'll be covered in flies. All they'll see is a cloud of flies coming over the hill.

BROTHER RAVEN
Yeah, and it'll be so stinky!

THEY ALL STARE AT HIM FOR A MOMENT. WOODEN WOMAN WALKS DOWNSTAGE. SHE TAKES OUT HER RED MARBLE AND STARES AT IT THROUGH THE LIGHT. SISTER COYOTE WALKS UP TO HER AND LIGHTS A CIGARETTE AND BLOWS THE SMOKE INTO THE AIR AND INTO THE LIGHT THAT WOODEN WOMAN IS STARING AT.

SISTER COYOTE
Did you smell the horses?

WOODEN WOMAN STOPS LOOKING THROUGH HER MARBLE AND PUTS IT AWAY.

WOODEN WOMAN
All I can smell is smoke

SISTER COYOTE
I couldn't smell the horses. I think those guys were just kidding about him smelling like horses. He did look pretty in that uniform and that big hat, they sure got big hats.

SISTER COYOTE OFFERS HER A DRAG FROM HER CIGARETTE.

SISTER COYOTE
Here, have a taste.

WOODEN WOMAN TAKES THE CIGARETTE AND TAKES A DRAG. SHE BLOWS THE SMOKE TOWARDS THE MEN.

WOODEN WOMAN
Everything becomes different when you look at it through smoke. Nothing is as clear as it should be, it looks older and worn.

SHE HANDS THE CIGARETTE BACK TO SISTER COYOTE.

WOODEN WOMAN
Thank you.

SISTER COYOTE
You're welcome.

SISTER COYOTE TAKES ANOTHER DRAG, BLOWS THE SMOKE AND LOOKS THROUGH IT TOWARDS THE MEN.

SISTER COYOTE
The smoke makes them disappear.

WOODEN WOMAN
I know, it's like they've never existed. One minute they're talking and smiling and the next they're gone.

WOODEN WOMAN GESTURES WITH THE RED MARBLE.

SISTER COYOTE
Wait till the smoke clears and then we can see and hear them again.

SHE PUTS OUT THE CIGARETTE AND THEY MOVE TO SET UP A GAME OF MARBLES. LIGHTS SHIFT TO THE MEN AT THE BENCH.

MISTER WOLF
I had a horse once.

BROTHER RAVEN
Was he fast?

MISTER WOLF
No, not really. He would just stand there and eat and shit.

WOODEN MAN
Doesn't sound like much of a horse.

MISTER WOLF
He wasn't. I won him at a card game. I had three queens. I bet all my belongings on that hand. There was no way I was going to let that horse get away from me. Three queens won me that horse.

BROTHER RAVEN
What did you bet for that horse?

MISTER WOLF
My life.

THE MUSICIAN PLAYS A RIFF. MISTER WOLF GIVES HIM A LOOK. THE MUSICIAN SHRUGS. MISTER WOLF TURNS BACK TO BROTHER RAVEN.

MISTER WOLF
I bet my life.

WOODEN MAN
What did you do that for? That sounds pretty dumb to me, betting your life on three queens.

MISTER WOLF
I wanted that horse. There was no way I was going to walk out of that game and have no horse. It was like nothing else mattered and the only way I could go on living was if I won that horse. So I put down my three queens, stood up, walked out the door, and I got on that horse and rode into the night.

BROTHER RAVEN
A horse is no good if he's not fast. What did you do with him?

MISTER WOLF
I rode him until the sun came up and then I sat there and just stared at him. He was one ugly horse.

WOODEN MAN
Three queens, your life, for an ugly horse?

MISTER WOLF
Yep. He was the ugliest animal I had ever seen. He only had one eye and his mouth sat there half open and his tongue hung out like a big snake.

MISTER WOLF PRETENDS TO BE THE HORSE WITH HIS TONGUE HANGING OUT, THEN SITS DOWN ON THE BENCH.

BROTHER RAVEN
I hate snakes. They're always trying to get me with their big teeth. Sometimes I can't get five steps without one of them trying to bite me. You ever been bitten by a snake?

WOODEN MAN
No, but I did get bit by a dog before. Big dog bit me on the ass. He wouldn't let go, just bit right into my ass and stared at me with crazy eyes.

BROTHER RAVEN
What did you do?

WOODEN MAN
I tried to spin him around and knock him off but he had a hold of me good. I spun and spun but he wouldn't let go. I stopped and looked down into his eyes, I tried to warn him to let go but he held on, so I took out my knife from my pocket and I stabbed him right in the ass. His eyes and mouth opened wide enough for me to get my ass out of his mouth. I turned around and showed him the piece of his ass that I had just cut out and told him that we were even and that he better get on down the road or I was going to cut him somewhere else. He turned and ran away leaving me there with my bloody knife and my bloody and sore ass.

WOODEN MAN SITS DOWN IN HIS SPOT VERY CAREFULLY AND ON ONE CHEEK.

BROTHER RAVEN
I've never been bitten by a dog but I have been bitten by a snake before.

MISTER WOLF
Yeah, but did he bite you in the ass?

BROTHER RAVEN
No, he bit me right on the heart.

HE LIFTS UP HIS SHIRT AND SHOWS BOTH MEN WHERE HE HAS BEEN BITTEN BY A SNAKE, THERE ARE BITE SCARS RIGHT WHERE HIS HEART IS.

WOODEN MAN
That's gotta hurt.

MISTER WOLF
How in the heck did you let a snake bite you on the heart like that?

BROTHER RAVEN
I didn't let him, he took a bite when I was sleeping right beside him.

WOODEN MAN
What were you doing sleeping beside a snake? I thought you hated snakes.

BROTHER RAVEN
I didn't back then, I thought he was ok, he gave me some of the chicken that he had stolen from some farmer. I thought, any snake who would give me some of their chicken must be a good snake.

MISTER WOLF
You ate raw chicken with a snake?

BROTHER RAVEN
No, he cooked it up, made a nice sauce out of some of the old berries that I had picked up along the road. We cooked it over a nice fire and sat there by the river and ate that chicken whole.

WOODEN MAN
And then he bit you on the heart?

BROTHER RAVEN
No, not right away. He told me stories about where he had come from and as it got later and later I began to fall asleep. He must've curled up beside me for warmth because I woke up one time and found him right there beside me. I didn't want to be rude and ask him to move away because he had given me his food and he had let me sleep by his fire. So I let him sleep there beside me, closed my eyes, and tried to dream.

WOODEN MAN
That's when he bit you.

BROTHER RAVEN
No, not right away.

WOODEN MAN
Geez, did he bite you at all or are you just making this story up?

BROTHER RAVEN
No, he bit me. But not right away. It was like he was trying to get close enough to me so he could bite right into my heart. I went back to sleep with him there beside me and then I woke up again and this time I found him right up my shirt and he had his head right next to my heart. I tapped him on top of the head and asked him what he was doing.

MISTER WOLF
What did he say?

BROTHER RAVEN
Nothing. He looked right up at me with those green eyes and he opened his mouth up real slow and then he bit right into my chest. I let out a scream and jumped up and tried to pull him off but he was under my shirt and I couldn't get a good grip on him so he bit harder and deeper. His teeth felt like they were razors cutting into my chest. I tore my shirt off and now I had a hold of him but still he wouldn't let go and all this time he looked at me with those green eyes and had those razor teeth buried into my chest. It was as if he was smiling to me. Smiling because he knew I was going to die.

BROTHER RAVEN
I pulled and pulled on him and it felt like I was stretching him. His eyes closed and he knew that he had to let go so he opened that big mouth and his teeth slowly came out of my chest and I swung him around in the air and I threw him into the river.

MISTER WOLF
Could he swim?

BROTHER RAVEN
Yes, he could swim. But not fast enough. When he hit the water the sound made a big splash and an owl who had been watching all this jumped from its tree and it glided towards the struggling snake.

BROTHER RAVEN CROSSES TO STAND BEHIND THE BENCH.

BROTHER RAVEN
All I could see were those green eyes as they tried to make it back to shore but that owl came down and snapped that snake in half.

BROTHER RAVEN PLAYFULLY GRABS THE MEN'S SHOULDERS, STARTLING THEM.

BROTHER RAVEN
Those green eyes closed one more time and disappeared with the owl as the night became quiet.

LIGHTS SHIFT TO SISTER COYOTE AND WOODEN WOMAN. THEY BEGIN TO PLAY MARBLES AS THE MEN BECOME WOODEN. SISTER COYOTE SHOOTS FIRST AND MISSES.

SISTER COYOTE
Wasn't much of a marble player.

WOODEN WOMAN
This is a magic marble, watch how it moves and takes the other marbles from the circle.

SHE TAKES OUT THE REST OF THE MARBLES AND SITS AND STARES AT THE RED MARBLE.

SISTER COYOTE
My brother used to play a lot of marbles. The other kids would save up their money until they could buy a couple of marbles at the reserve store. They would come by all ready to take on my brother because he was the champ.

WOODEN WOMAN
Did he have a marble like this one?

SISTER COYOTE
No. But he had the magic within him. The other kids would watch as he gracefully took their favorite marbles. They watched as he took the marbles they had saved up for.

WOODEN WOMAN
Did anyone ever beat him?

SISTER COYOTE
They say he beat himself.

WOODEN WOMAN
What do you mean?

SISTER COYOTE
He had won all the marbles on the reserve and no one would play with him anymore. So he gathered up all his marbles and he went into the woods to play one final game with someone who had a chance to beat him.

WOODEN WOMAN
Who did he play against?

SISTER COYOTE
They say the spirits came to his game and they brought all their magic marbles. My brother played each one until all their marbles were now his.

WOODEN WOMAN
What did he do with all those magic marbles?

SISTER COYOTE
Some say he gives them to children who have nothing. He comes late at night and leaves one red marble on their chest. When they wake up, find it, they know that my brother's spirit has come to see them.

WOODEN WOMAN HOLDS THE RED MARBLE UP TO THE LIGHT.

WOODEN WOMAN
See how the light makes it glow?

SISTER COYOTE
One red marble.

WOODEN WOMAN
See the life, the power?

SISTER COYOTE
It looks like a tiny heart.

WOODEN WOMAN
A child's heart.

WOODEN WOMAN AND SISTER COYOTE STARE AT IT THROUGH THE LIGHT AS STAGE LIGHTS FADE.

THERE IS MUSIC HERE. IN DIM LIGHT, A PICNIC BASKET AND BABY ARE BROUGHT ONTO STAGE . WE HEAR A BABY CRY SOFLTLY AS BROTHER RAVEN HANDS THE BABY TO WOODEN WOMAN. WOODEN WOMAN CRADLES THE CHILD GENTLY, THEN SITS ON THE BENCH AND HANDS HER TO WOODEN MAN.

SCENE 7 – DAYTIME

LIGHTS UP AS MUSIC FINISHES. MISTER WOLF, SISTER COYOTE, AND BROTHER RAVEN ARE SITTING ON THE ROCK WITH THE PICNIC BASKET AND FOOD. WOODEN WOMAN AND WOODEN MAN ARE SITTING ON THE BENCH. WOODEN MAN IS HOLDING THE BABY IN HIS ARMS. OFFSTAGE WE HEAR CHILDREN PLAYING IN A PARK.

WOODEN MAN
She's so pretty. Look at those brown eyes.

WOODEN WOMAN
What should we call her?

WOODEN MAN
We should wait for the Spirits to show us what we should call her.

WOODEN WOMAN
She likes it here, see how she smiles.

WOODEN MAN
Let's listen to the spirits and see what name we should give to our daughter.

MISTER WOLF TAKES OFF HIS DIRTY RUNNING SHOES AND BEGINS TO PICK AT HIS TOES.

MISTER WOLF
Look at these toes. Have you ever seen more perfect toes before?

BROTHER RAVEN
They look more like claws.

BROTHER RAVEN TAKES OFF HIS SHOES AND SHOWS HIS FOOT TO MISTER WOLF.

BROTHER RAVEN
Now these are perfect feet.

SISTER COYOTE
They look more like turkey feet, all skinny and hairy.

BROTHER RAVEN
These are great feet. I can pick anything up with these.

BROTHER RAVEN PLAYS AT PICKING UP HIS SOCK.

WOODEN MAN
Turkey Feet!

WOODEN WOMAN
What?

WOODEN MAN
We can call her Turkey Feet.

WOODEN WOMAN
Turkey Feet? I don't think so.

WOODEN MAN
You're right, the other children would laugh at her.

BROTHER RAVEN TOSSES HIS SOCK ONTO MISTER WOLF'S HEAD. THEY ALL LAUGH. SISTER COYOTE TAKES OFF HER SHOES AND PUTS HER FEET IN THE AIR.

SISTER COYOTE
My feet are perfect.

MISTER WOLF
Never seen a perfect foot before, let me see.

HE STANDS AND EXAMINES HER FEET.

MISTER WOLF
You should see these, they're perfect.

BROTHER RAVEN LEANS IN AND EXAMINES HER FEET.

BROTHER RAVEN
They're perfect.

HE BEGINS TO TICKLE HER FEET.

SISTER COYOTE
Hey, cut that out, it tickles.

BROTHER RAVEN AND MISTER WOLF BOTH TICKLE HER FEET AS SHE SCREAMS AND LAUGHS.

SISTER COYOTE
Don't! Hey, stop! I'll pee myself!

THEY BOTH STOP TICKLING HER AND SHE TRIES TO CATCH HER BREATH.

SISTER COYOTE
You guys are so mean.

MISTER WOLF
Just having some fun.

BROTHER RAVEN
We were just playing. No harm done. Are you ok? I mean, did you pee yourself?

SISTER COYOTE
No. But I bet I can tickle you until you pee your pants.

SHE GOES TO HIM AND TICKLES HIS SIDES AS HE SQUIRMS TO GET AWAY.

BROTHER RAVEN
Don't! Ravens don't like to be tickled. Hey, stop it! You're ruffling my feathers.

SHE STOPS AND GOES AND TRIES TO TICKLE MISTER WOLF, BUT HE JUST SITS THERE AND IGNORES HER.

MISTER WOLF
You can't tickle a wolf.

SHE STOPS AND SITS DOWN.

WOODEN MAN
Ruffled Feather!

WOODEN WOMAN
What?

WOODEN MAN
We can call her Ruffled Feather.

WOODEN WOMAN
I don't think so. She is much more beautiful than a ruffled feather.

SHE TAKES THE BABY FROM WOODEN MAN AND HOLDS IT IN HER ARMS.

WOODEN MAN
You're right. Boy, these spirits sure aren't very good with choosing a name.

OFFSTAGE WE HEAR CHILDREN PLAYING AND THEN A VOICE SAYING: "GET OUT OF HERE, YOU STINKING KID." TOURIST ENTERS DRESSED AS A SMALL BOY WEARING A PROPELLER CAP. TOURIST GOES UP TO WOODEN WOMAN AND PULLS ON HER HAIR. THEY BOTH DO NOT REACT. TOURIST GOES UP TO WOODEN MAN AND KICKS HIM IN THE SHIN. TOURIST GOES TO PICNIC AREA AND STARES AT MISTER WOLF, SISTER COYOTE, AND BROTHER RAVEN. WOODEN MAN REACHES FOR THE TOURIST BUT WOODEN WOMAN PULLS HIM BACK.

WOODEN MAN
Rotten kid.

WOODEN WOMAN
Leave him be, he doesn't know any better.

WOODEN MAN
Just a good kick in the ass. That's all it'll take.

WOODEN WOMAN
He doesn't know any better.

WOODEN MAN
Where do they learn that?

WOODEN WOMAN
History, I guess.

TOURIST GOES AND POKES MISTER WOLF. MISTER WOLF HOWLS AND TRIES TO BE BIG AND STRONG.

MISTER WOLF
You better get away from me kid. I'm a big bad wolf!

TOURIST SPEAKS AS A SNOTTY KID.

TOURIST
Wolves don't wear suits.

MISTER WOLF
Oh yeah?

TOURIST
Yeah. Wolves have big teeth and walk on all fours.

MISTER WOLF
Well, I don't.

TOURIST
Then you're not a wolf.

MISTER WOLF
Beat it, kid, before I bite you on the ass and show you just how big my teeth are.

MISTER WOLF REACHES FOR HIM BUT THE TOURIST IS NOW INTERESTED IN BROTHER RAVEN AND RUNS TOWARD HIM. BROTHER RAVEN TRIES TO FLAP HIS ARMS LIKE WINGS.

BROTHER RAVEN
You better not mess with me, I'm a big old raven and I'll peck out your eyes if you're not careful.

TOURIST
You're not a raven. Ravens don't have greasy hair, they have beautiful black feathers.

BROTHER RAVEN
Yeah, well I'm having a bad hair day. Get going or I'll...

HE REACHES FOR HIM BUT TOURIST RUNS AWAY AND GOES TO SISTER COYOTE AND PULLS ON HER HAIR.

SISTER COYOTE
Ouch! Hey, quit it!

TOURIST
What're you going to do about it?

SISTER COYOTE
I'll bite you! I'm a coyote and my bite really hurts!

TOURIST
You're no coyote. Coyotes are beautiful and have nice eyes.

SISTER COYOTE
I have nice eyes. Hey, where do you get off telling me I don't have nice eyes?

TOURIST SMILES AND LEANS IN AS IF TO STROKE HER, BUT INSTEAD PULLS ON HER HAIR AGAIN, THEN HE SKIPS OFF STAGE. SISTER COYOTE BEGINS TO CRY.

SISTER COYOTE
I have nice eyes, don't I?

BROTHER RAVEN AND MISTER WOLF GO UP TO HER AND TRY TO CONSOLE HER.

BROTHER RAVEN
Sure you do.

MISTER WOLF
Nothing more beautiful than a coyote's eyes.

BROTHER RAVEN
Except maybe her feet.

MISTER WOLF
And her feet.

SISTER COYOTE
Thanks guys.

BROTHER RAVEN
My eyes are black like the night.

MISTER WOLF
My eyes are yellow like the sun.

SISTER COYOTE
My mother told me that my eyes were like the earth and they could look at you forever. That's what she used to call me, Forever.

SISTER COYOTE CROSSES TOWARD THE BENCH, LOST IN THOUGHT. BROTHER RAVEN AND MISTER WOLF JOIN HER. THEY GAZE INTO THE NIGHT.

WOODEN MAN GIVES WOODEN WOMAN A KISS AND STARES AT HIS CHILD AS WOODEN WOMAN HOLDS HER IN HER ARMS.

WOODEN MAN
We shall call her Forever.

WOODEN WOMAN
Yes, that's a wonderful name.

WOODEN MAN
Look at those eyes.

WOODEN WOMAN
Yes, they look at you forever.

LIGHTS FADE

SCENE 8 - DAYTIME

THE STAGE IS COVERED IN DEAD LEAVES. SISTER COYOTE, BROTHER RAVEN AND MISTER WOLF ARE STANDING AT THE EDGE OF THE BENCH. WOODEN WOMAN IS STILL HOLDING THE CHILD IN HER ARMS AND WOODEN MAN SITS BESIDE HER. OFFSTAGE WE HEAR A MILITARY BUGLE PLAYING SOFTLY AND THEN THE SOUND OF A MARCHING DRUM, SOUNDS OF MEN GOING INTO BATTLE. TOURIST ENTERS NOW DRESSED IN A BLUE U.S. CALVARY UNIFORM. HE IS HOLDING FRESHLY TAKEN SCALPS, HIS OLD CAMERA AND TRIPOD. HE PLACES THE SCALPS IN THE HANDS OF WOODEN MAN AND WOODEN WOMAN, GOES AND TAKES THEIR PICTURE. NO ONE MOVES. TOURIST GATHERS THE SCALPS, HIS CAMERA AND TRIPOD, AND EXITS AS STAGE LIGHTS AND SOUNDS FADE.

SCENE 9

DAYTIME ON THE ROCK. SISTER COYOTE, BROTHER RAVEN AND MISTER WOLF CROSS TO THE ROCK AND BEGIN TO ENJOY A PICNIC. OFFSTAGE WE HEAR: "GET OUT OF HERE, YOU STINKING INDIAN." WOODEN MAN STANDS AND FACES DOWNSTAGE.

WOODEN MAN
We are going into battle.

WOODEN WOMAN STANDS WITH HER CHILD STILL IN HER ARMS AND FACES DOWNSTAGE.

WOODEN WOMAN
The men have all left the village.

MISTER WOLF
This bread is real tasty.

SISTER COYOTE
Could you pass the butter? I like a lot of butter on my bread.

BROTHER RAVEN
Here you go. Could you pass the blue berries? It's been a long time since I've had any.

MISTER WOLF
It's a nice day for a picnic. Sun's out, not a cloud in the sky.

MORE LEAVES FALL TO THE GROUND. WE HEAR SOUNDS OF WAR SOFTLY IN THE DISTANCE: HORSES, MEN SCREAMING, GUN FIRE, SCREAMS OF WOUNDED AND DYING MEN. IT BECOMES EVENING AND THE SKY TURNS RED.

WOODEN MAN
I must go. I must kill those that have killed my fathers.

WOODEN WOMAN
The men have all left. It's just the mothers and the children. Don't go! Don't go! They will kill you and there will be no more fathers for our children. Don't go! Our baby has only lived two days and has not met the earth and all its beauty.

WOODEN MAN
I must go. I must kill those that have killed my mothers.

WOODEN WOMAN IS HOLDING HER CHILD IN HER ARMS AS SOUNDS OF BATTLE GET LOUDER AND LOUDER.

WOODEN WOMAN
Come back! Come back! Be with us forever. We can hide in the forest and the soldiers will not find us. Come back! Come back!

WOODEN MAN
I must go. I must kill those that have killed my children.

MUSICIAN
Chichelh Siya:m. (Supreme Being.)

WOODEN MAN & MUSICIAN
Ey Chap te Sqelwel. (Keeping a good mind.)

WOODEN MAN RUNS OFFSTAGE AS IF GOING OFF TO BATTLE. SOUNDS BUILD TO A CRASHING END - AS WOODEN WOMAN STANDS, STARING INTO THE EMPTY SPACE WITH HER CHILD IN HER ARMS.

WOODEN WOMAN
The men have all disappeared. The Blue Coats have taken and destroyed their lives. The earth has become silent. No more screams, no more screams. It's quiet now, my child. Sleep and dream, sleep and dream of days unlike this, this is a sad day, a day filled with the loss of our men. May their spirits sleep like you, my child. May they sleep with endless peace.

LIGHTS SHIFT BACK TO DAYTIME ON THE ROCK.

MISTER WOLF
It's a great day for a picnic. Not one sound, not even noisy songbirds.

BROTHER RAVEN
You got something against birds.

MISTER WOLF
Only ones who sing poorly.

BROTHER RAVEN
(He tries to sing.) I wasn't much of a singer.

SISTER COYOTE
Could you pass the bread? My belly isn't quite full yet.

LIGHTS FADE IN PICNIC AREA.

SCENE 10

MISTER WOLF, BROTHER RAVEN, AND SISTER COYOTE ARE ASLEEP ON THE ROCK. WOODEN WOMAN STANDS ON THE EDGE OF THE PLATFORM STAGE LEFT HOLDING HER CHILD. TOURIST ENTERS. HE IS NOW DRESSED AS A MOVIE DIRECTOR.

TOURIST
Lights! Camera. Action!

WOODEN MAN ENTERS DOWN THE AISLE RUNNING.

TOURIST
Ok, bring in the buffalo!

WOODEN MAN
The cannons fired and the earth shook as they charged towards us with their fire.

WOODEN WOMAN TALKS TO HER CHILD.

WOODEN WOMAN
Your father was the bravest of all the men. He held his head up high when he went into battle with those blue coats.

TOURIST
More smoke! I need more smoke!

WOODEN MAN
The cannons killed half the men in five minutes. We had no where to run. My brothers were on the ground, torn and dying by that screaming hot metal.

WOODEN WOMAN
Your father was a great man, everyone listened when he spoke, they looked up to him and they respected his vision.

TOURIST
Ok, kill the buffalo! Where's the wolf? Someone get the wolf out of his trailer. I need the wolf to howl on cue. Can he do that?

MISTER WOLF HOWLS IN HIS SLEEP.

WOODEN WOMAN
Your father was so beautiful. His eyes held my spirit the first time I looked into them.

WOODEN MAN
A piece of hot metal cut into my leg and I fell from my horse as those around me died.

TOURIST TALKS DIRECTLY TO WOODEN MAN.

TOURIST
Could you talk slower? More poetically. Slowly and clearly. These words were written for a reason. Let's hear them, ok? More cannon fire! More cannon fire!

WOODEN MAN

I was there on the ground with my leg bleeding and burning with the fire of those men who were here to destroy us. My brothers had all died and I watched their spirits rise off the ground and into the beautiful sky. They gathered above the battle and did not know what to do. They were confused and they began to cry and sing like the death that they had become.

TOURIST

Ok, that's better. Now, I want you to look mean. Can we see your War face? Who did this guy's make-up? I want more paint! More paint on this one! Make-up! Make-up!

WOODEN MAN

I was alone as the soldiers charged forward with the cold steel of their bayonets. They slid the blades so easily into my brothers who were already dead. The cold blade slid into the warmth of death and then they cut off their beautiful hair. With the harshness of a cold blade they took their hair and screamed in victory. My brothers screamed from the sky as their hair was taken and shown to them and then the battle became quiet…

TOURIST

Ok, enough of this shot.

WOODEN MAN EXITS.

TOURIST

Let's get some close-ups of those bleeding scalps. I want them to drip and drip. And get the women and children ready, I want to see the children and the women screaming and crying. Can they do that? Tell them we'll pay them more if there's real tears. Ok, let's go! Let's not waste this beautiful sunny day.

TOURIST EXITS. WOODEN WOMAN STANDS ON THE EDGE OF THE PLATFORM AS LIGHTS SLOWLY BEGIN TO FADE.

WOODEN WOMAN

The soldiers didn't stop. They were heading for our village. They were coming to kill us all and take our hair. They were coming to kill our children so they would not grow up and avenge the death of their fathers. The spirits of the dead men had made it back to the village before the soldiers. They were above us and they were telling us to run to the forest. Where are you, Husband? I do not hear your voice. Where are you!? Wake up children! Wake up! We must run to the forest and hide! Wake up!

WOODEN WOMAN TRIES TO WAKE UP THE SLEEPING MISTER WOLF, BROTHER RAVEN, AND SISTER COYOTE, BUT THEY STAY ASLEEP AS THE LIGHT FADES.

SCENE 11 – EVENING

IT IS DAWN FOR THE CHILDREN, WHO ARE ALL SITTING ON THE FRONT OF THE ROCK. WOODEN WOMAN IS STANDING BEHIND THE BENCH WITH HER CHILD IN HER ARMS. OFFSTAGE WE HEAR: "GET OUT OF HERE, YOU STINKING BLACK ROBE." TOURIST ENTERS NOW DRESSED AS A PRIEST. HE SETS UP HIS EASEL AND BEGINS TO PAINT A PICTURE. WOODEN WOMAN BEGINS TO MOVE AND SPEAK.

WOODEN WOMAN
Your father is dead. The soldiers are here. They are killing the women and children.

SISTER COYOTE
I hate waiting for the bus.

BROTHER RAVEN
Me too.

MISTER WOLF
This bus is always late.

WOODEN WOMAN
The soldiers took the children and they made them watch as they shot all the women. My sisters fell to the ground as their children screamed for them. The soldiers took the hair of my sisters and then they turned on the children. I had run into the forest with my child and I watched as the soldiers walked to the crying children. What had they done? Why did they want to kill the children?

THE TOURIST GOES TO SISTER COYOTE AND TAKES HER HAND.

SISTER COYOTE
When I was a child I was sent to a Catholic school on a bus. My mother was screaming at the priests and the nuns. She didn't want me to go with them.

THE TOURIST HELPS HER STAND.

WOODEN WOMAN
The soldiers took each child by the hand and they led them to a hole. "Don't kill them!" I wanted to scream but they would see where I was hiding and they would kill my child. So I stayed quiet but in my head I screamed, "Don't take them! Don't kill our children!"

THE TOURIST GUIDES SISTER COYOTE DOWNSTAGE.

SISTER COYOTE
I went with the sisters and the priests. I went to their schools and they cut my hair and told me to speak English. They told me that I was a savage and that the word of God would be my savior.

TOURIST CROSSES TO BROTHER RAVEN AND TAKES HIM BY THE ARM AS HE STANDS AND SPEAKS.

BROTHER RAVEN
I was taken away from my mother on a bus because the government men said she was unfit to care for me. I was sent to live with a family far, far away from home.

WOODEN WOMAN
They slit their throats, the youngest of the children, slit their throats and tossed their small harmless bodies into the hole.

TOURIST GIVES BROTHER RAVEN A PUSH DOWNSTAGE.

BROTHER RAVEN
My mother was too drunk to realize what was happening to me. The government men came and took me away, took me to a family that would never love me.

TOURIST CROSSES TO MISTER WOLF AND TAKES HIS HANDS BEHIND HIS BACK.

MISTER WOLF
I was sent to prison on a bus. Sent to rot behind cold bars for a crime I did not commit. They came to my grandmother's house and they took me to their prison.

TOURIST LEADS HIM DOWNSTAGE AS GREEN UPLIGHTS FROM THE LOWER PLATFORM COME UP ON ALL THREE. TOURIST RETURNS TO THE EASEL AND CONTINUES TO PAINT.

WOODEN WOMAN
The soldiers took the older children and dragged them towards the hole. They were screaming and begging for their lives but the soldiers shot them, each one with a bullet to the head. They tossed their lifeless bodies into the hole. The hole began to fill with blood.

MISTER WOLF
I couldn't stand it in there, with those steel bars keeping me away from my home, keeping me away from my grandmother.

BROTHER RAVEN
I couldn't stay there. I couldn't stay with a family that didn't want me. They never loved me. They never saw me as one of their own. But they were getting extra money from the government so they had to keep me. They had to keep me. They kept me in a little room beside the kitchen. They gave me bits of food but nothing a real raven needs to grow strong. I was getting to be a real nice bird before they got their hands on me. Look at me now, all skin and bones, you can't fly right if you're nothing but skin and bones, I tried to tell them, but they wouldn't listen to me. I am Raven, I would tell them but they kept me in that little room until I decided that I had had enough.

SISTER COYOTE
They kept me in that school, they kept me until I decided that I had had enough. I had had enough of being beaten and kicked around. I am a Coyote, I would scream at them but they would laugh and kick me some more. I am Coyote! But they would say that I was a child of God and that he would be my savior. I am Coyote! And I wasn't going to be kicked around anymore.

WOODEN WOMAN
My child began to cry. It was as if this child could feel the death around her. She began to cry louder than the sound of the soldiers as they yelled in victory. A soldier spotted me as I tried to run deeper into the forest.

SISTER COYOTE
My last night on earth was in my tiny bed. I was trying to dream of my family back home. The fat priest came into my room and he pulled off my little dress and he placed his fat cold body on top of me and he hurt me real bad, all the time telling me that I was his gift from the lord and that I should never tell anyone. He raped me and then he smacked me across the face and told me to never tell anyone or else God would punish me.

BROTHER RAVEN
My last night on earth was spent in my tiny room just beside the kitchen. The father of the family came into my room and told me that I had made a mess and that he would therefore have to punish me for this. I tried to tell him that I wasn't the one who made the mess but he came at me anyways. He took off his thick black belt and he tore off my little pants and he smacked me until I was bleeding and screaming for him to stop. He told me to never tell the government men about what he did to me or else I would never see my mother alive again.

MISTER WOLF
My last night on earth was spent in a dark cell. I hadn't eaten in days and they were telling me that they were going to keep me here until I was dead. They came into my cell and they beat me with pipes until I could no longer walk. They told me I would never see my grandmother again.

WOODEN WOMAN
The soldiers couldn't see me but they could hear my child crying. "Hush, little girl. Go to sleep. Hush, now." But she wouldn't stop crying. I took my hand and I placed it over her mouth but you could still hear her crying and the soldiers were getting closer and closer.

SISTER COYOTE
The fat priest left the piece of rope that he used for a belt in my tiny room. I placed the rope around my neck and tied it to the beam that went across my room.

WOODEN WOMAN
The soldiers began to shoot in the direction that I was hiding.

THE MUSICIAN MAKES A LOUD "GUNSHOT" SOUND.

SISTER COYOTE
I jumped and I became the Coyote.

SHE CROUCHES IN HER COYOTE POSITION AND FREEZES.

BROTHER RAVEN
The father of the family that never loved me left his thick black belt in my tiny room that was beside the kitchen. I placed the belt around my neck and placed the belt around the beam that cut across my tiny room.

WOODEN WOMAN
They were shooting right at me, one of the bullets ripped into a tree that was right near my head.

ANOTHER LOUD "GUNSHOT" IS HEARD.

BROTHER RAVEN
I jumped and I became the Raven.

HE RAISES HIS ARMS LIKE WINGS, TAKES HIS RAVEN POSITION AND FREEZES.

MISTER WOLF
They placed the noose around my neck. The priest said some words to me that I couldn't understand. He didn't even look me in the eyes. He turned away and they let me fall.

WOODEN WOMAN
Another bullet hit me in the arm and I screamed real loud and my child began to scream. Another bullet hit the tree again.

ANOTHER LOUD "GUNSHOT" IS HEARD.

MISTER WOLF
I jumped and I became the Wolf.

HE TAKES HIS WOLF POSITION AND FREEZES. AFTER A MOMENT, THE THREE SPIRITS STEP OFF. THEY LIE DOWN AND PULL DIRT-COLORED BLANKETS HAPHAZARDLY ON TOP OF THEMSELVES.

TOURIST CROSSES DOWNSTAGE, ADMINISTERS THE LAST RITES FOR EACH, GATHERS HIS EASEL AND EXITS.

WOODEN WOMAN
They were coming to kill me and take my hair. My child wouldn't stop screaming so I took some dead leaves and I gently pushed them into her mouth.

WOODEN WOMAN BENDS DOWN AND TAKES DEAD LEAVES AND PLACES THEM INTO THE MOUTH OF HER CHILD.

WOODEN WOMAN
There now, my child. You can sleep now. The soldiers can't hear you
anymore. Sleep, my child. Sleep and dream of days unlike this one. Dream
of days spent playing and enjoying this earth that was given to us by the
Creator. Sleep and dream my child.

**LIGHTS FADE AS WOODEN WOMAN CROUCHES BEHIND THE
BENCH WITH HER CHILD. THE MUSICIAN PLAYS SOFTLY.**

SCENE 12 – DAYTIME

**WOODEN MAN AND WOODEN WOMAN ARE SITTING IN THEIR
SPOTS ON THE BENCH. OFFSTAGE WE HEAR: "GET OUT OF
HERE, YOU STINKING TOURIST." TOURIST ENTERS, NOW
DRESSED IN MODERN CLOTHING. HE CROSSES THE LOWER
PLATFORM, STEPPING OVER THE THREE. HE THEN SETS UP
HIS CAMERA AND TRIPOD AND TRIES TO SET THE TIMER.
NOTHING HAPPENS. TOURIST CHECKS THE CAMERA AND THE
FILM FALLS OUT. TOURIST GATHERS THE FILM, CAMERA AND
TRIPOD AND EXITS.**

WOODEN MAN
It sure is quiet here without the children.

WOODEN WOMAN
Weather's changing. The fall's almost over.

WOODEN MAN
Are you warm enough?

WOODEN WOMAN
Yes. Are you?

WOODEN MAN
Sure. Not too much wind on this side.

WOODEN WOMAN
Are you hungry? I've got some apple left.

WOODEN MAN
No, my belly's full.

SISTER COYOTE, BROTHER RAVEN AND MISTER WOLF BEGIN TO HUM A CHILDRENS TUNE FROM BENEATH THE BLANKETS.

WOODEN WOMAN
I didn't mean to kill her.

WOODEN MAN
I know.

WOODEN WOMAN
She wouldn't stop crying. Everything I did made her cry louder.

WOODEN MAN
I know. It's ok. It's over now. We just have to live on, together.

WOODEN WOMAN
I just wanted her to be quiet for a moment so I could think straight. I never wanted her to die like that.

WOODEN MAN
We still have each other. We still have our memories.

WOODEN WOMAN STANDS AND STARES AT THE LEAVES.

WOODEN WOMAN
I put leaves into her mouth so she would be silent just for a moment. She stopped crying when I did that. I was able to breathe for a moment and rest and try and get strong, but she wouldn't wake up when I was taking the leaves out of her mouth. She just stayed there all quiet and so beautiful.

WOODEN MAN STANDS AND EMBRACES HER.

WOODEN MAN
Rest now. She is with the spirits of the forest. They will take care of her now.

WOODEN WOMAN
I loved her so much. I would do anything to bring her back, you know that don't you?

WOODEN MAN
Yes, I do. Rest now. She is with the spirits. Can you hear them playing?

BROTHER RAVEN, SISTER COYOTE AND MISTER WOLF SING SOFTLY FROM BENEATH THEIR COVERINGS.

BROTHER RAVEN, SISTER COYOTE & MISTER WOLF
Mickey Mouse, Minne Mouse, Pluto too.
They're all stars at Disneyland
Disneyland, Disneyland
They're all stars at Disneyland
Hey-ya, hey-yo.

WOODEN WOMAN
Little child with her little red heart. She would've grown up to be a wonderful daughter. Her little red heart and those brown eyes that looked up at you forever.

WOODEN MAN
I love you more than anything on this earth. I will never leave you alone again. Let's just sit here a while longer and go home. The weather's changing and soon the snow will come.

WOODEN WOMAN
I am at peace here. I can see her, you know. I can see her as a little girl playing with other children. I can see her playing catch with her brothers, I can see her as she plays marbles and gets dirty, I can see her as she becomes a woman, I can see her as she becomes a spirit, a beautiful spirit upon this earth.

WOODEN MAN
Rest now. We will come back tomorrow and see what spirits come to visit us. Go to sleep, my love. Sleep and dream of days like this. Days filled with wonderful and alive spirits that play and sing, forever...

THE MUSICIAN PLAYS SOFTLY AS LIGHTS SLOWLY FADE TO BLACK.

END

About the Author

Joseph A. Dandurand (Kwantlen First Nation) is from British Columbia. He is a poet, playwright, fisherman, researcher, archaeologist, and proud father. Playwright -in-residence for the Museum of Civilization in Hull in 1995 and for Native Earth in Toronto in 1996, his produced plays include *Crackers and Soup* (1994), *No Totem for My Story* (1995), *Where Two Rivers Meet* (1995), and *Please Do Not Touch the Indians* (2004). He has also authored a radio script, *St Mary's*, produced by CBC Radio in 1999. His poems have appeared in numerous journals and anthologies and are collected in *Upside Down Raven*, *I Touched the Coyote's Tongue*, and *burning for the dead and scratching for the poor* and *looking into the eyes of my forgotten dreams*. His essay X. ALATSEP (WRITTEN DOWN) appeared in *Genocide of the Mind: New Native Writings,* and his most recent book is *Shake.*

To order additional copies of this book and/or to receive permission to conduct a production of this play, please contact the following:

rENEGADE pLANETS pUBLISHING
PO Box 2493
Candler, NC 28715
Ph: 828.665.7630
Fax: 828.670.6347
Email: renegadepl@aol.com
www.marijomoore.com